7/04

D1193698

Hodder Toddler

This book belongs to:

....

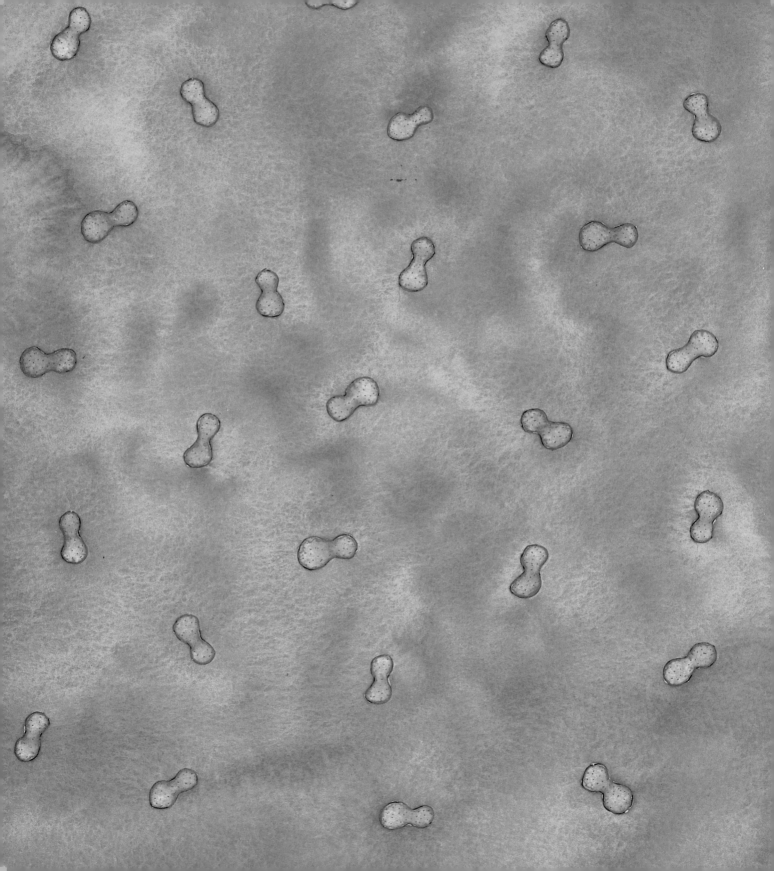

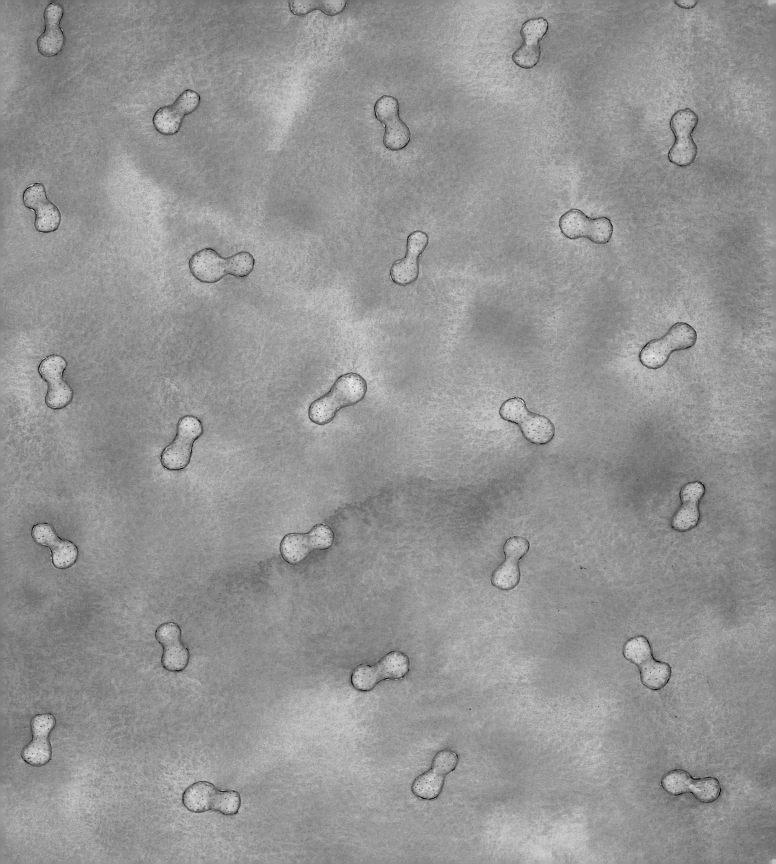

Hello Thomas Louis — R.A.

For Sasha and Tony and Sophia — D.H.

HELLO PEANUT!
by Rachel Anderson and Debbie Harter

British Library Cataloguing in Publication Data
A catalogue record of this book is available from the British Library.

ISBN 0 340 85248 8 (PB)

Text copyright © Rachel Anderson 2003
Illustration copyright © Debbie Harter 2003

First edition published 2003
10 9 8 7 6 5 4 3 2 1

Published by Hodder Children's Books
a division of Hodder Headline Limited
338 Euston Road London NW1 3BH

Printed in Hong Kong

Hello Peanut!

Written by Rachel Anderson

Illustrated by Debbie Harter

Hodder
Children's
Books

A division of Hodder Headline Limited

How big is the baby?

As big as a dot.

How big is the baby?

As big as a peanut.

Hello Peanut!
Want to share my sandwich?

How big is the baby?

As big as a tadpole.

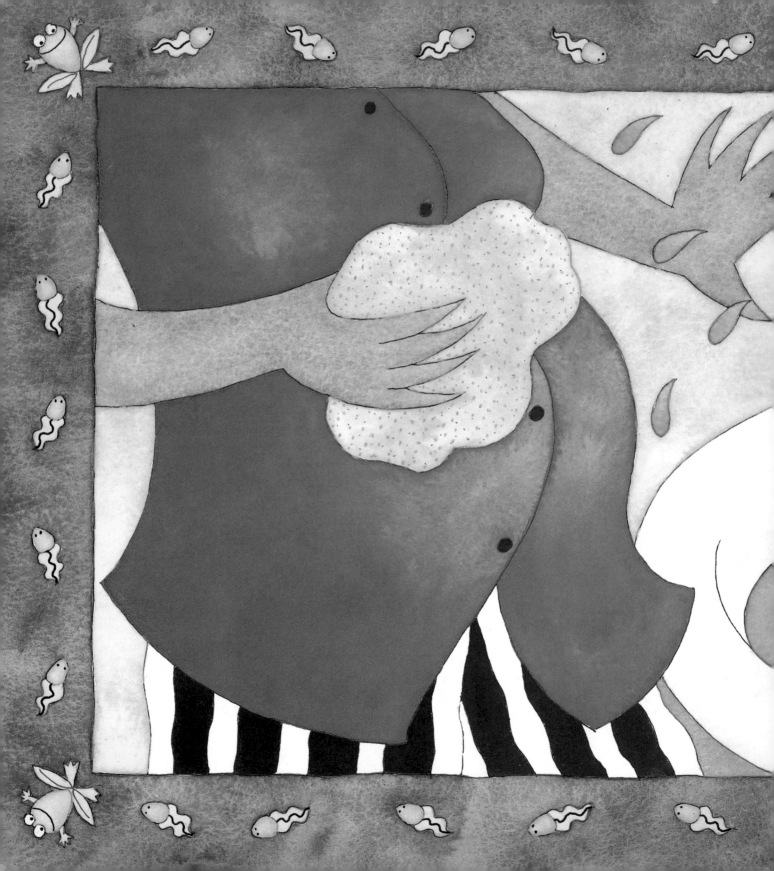

How big is the baby?

As big as a dormouse.

How big is the baby?

As big as an elephant.

Good day to you, Ellie!
Want to play heffalumps?

Where's my mum?

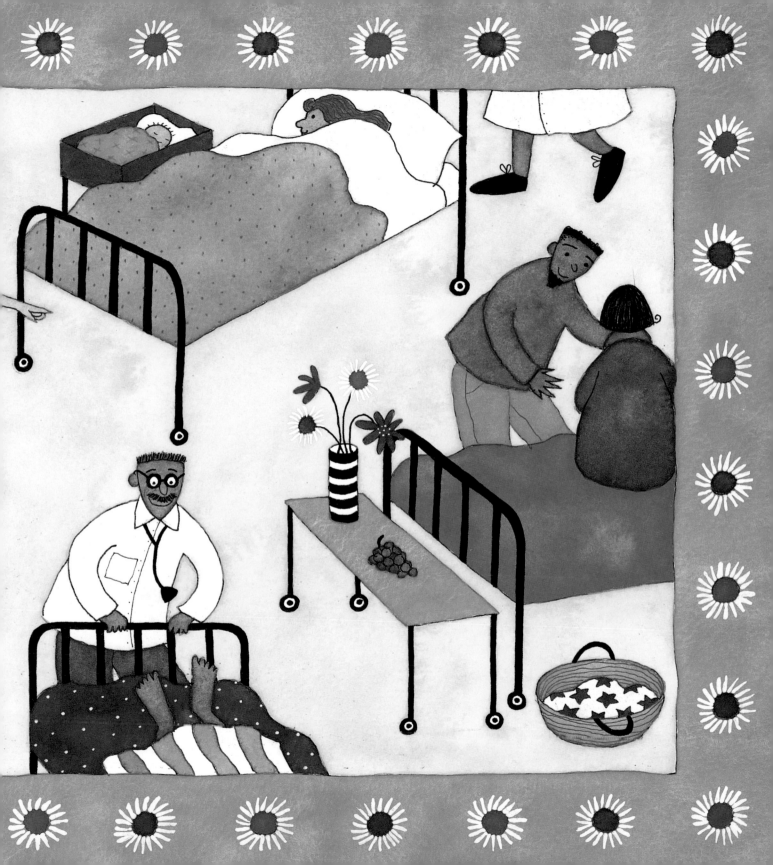

Hello tiny brother.

Welcome to my world.

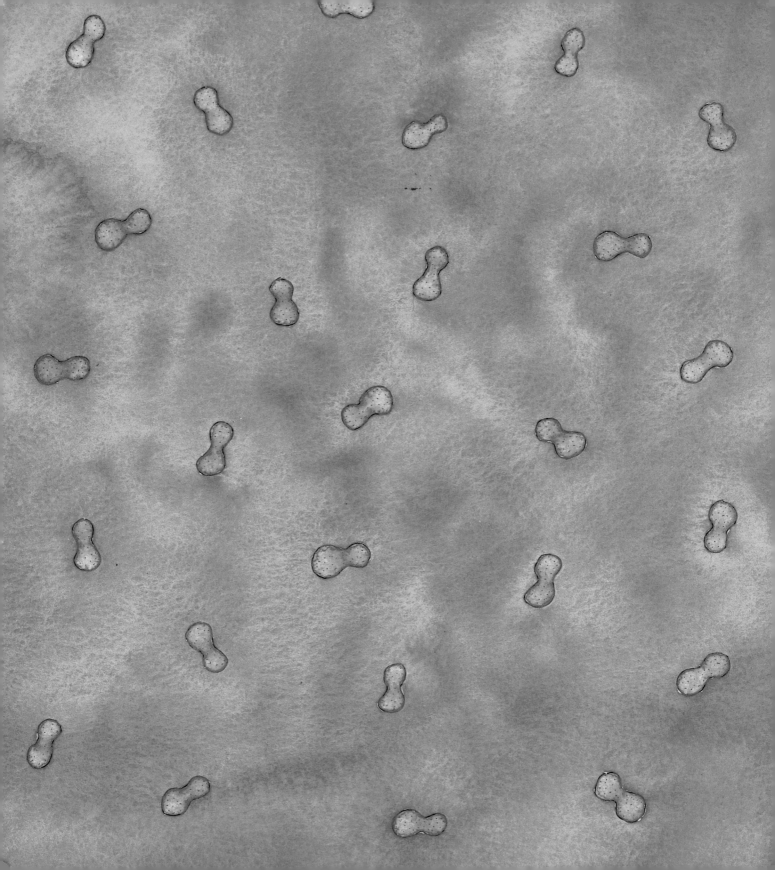

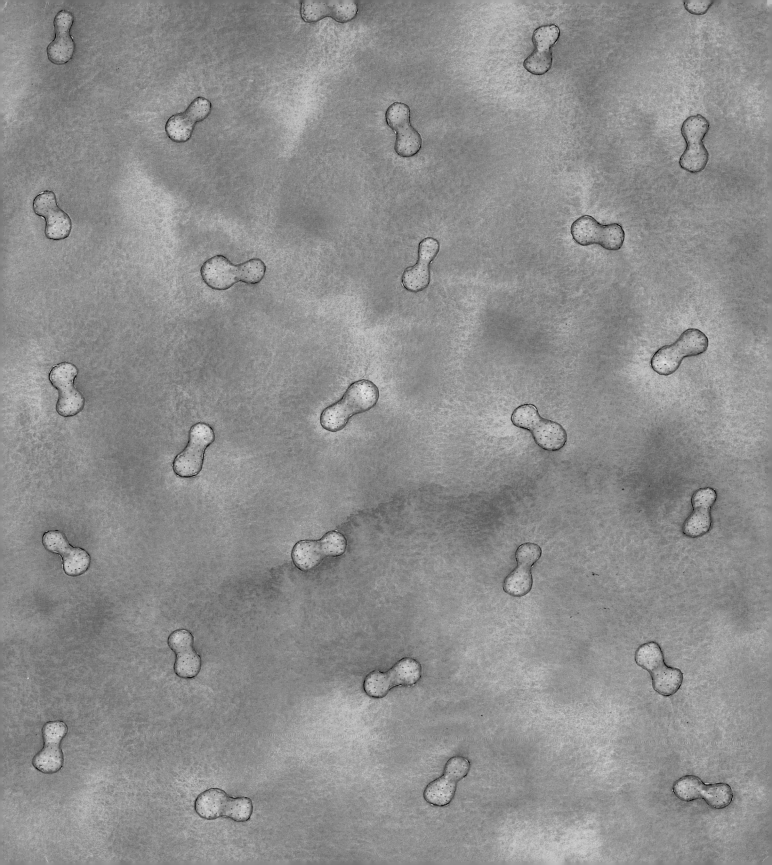

Goodbye
Hodder Toddler